DEC 19 2013

35444001642569
j HOW
Howard, Kate.
Scooby-Doo! stage fright
: a junior novelization

Scooby-Doo!

Stage Fright

A Junior Novelization

DI019033

SCOOBY-DOO!

Stage Fright
A Junior Novelization

Thompson-Nicola Regional District
Library System
300 - 465 VICTORIA STREET
KAMLOOPS, B.C.   V2C 2A9

Adapted by Kate Howard
Based upon the script written by Doug Langdale

WORLDWIDE PUBLISHING

SCHOLASTIC INC.

If you purchased this book without a cover, you should be aware that this book is stolen property. It was reported as "unsold and destroyed" to the publisher, and neither the author nor the publisher has received any payment for this "stripped book."

No part of this publication may be reproduced in whole or in part, stored in a retrieval system, or transmitted in any form or by any means, electronic, mechanical, photocopying, recording, or otherwise, without written permission of the publisher. For information regarding permission, write to Scholastic Inc., Attention: Permissions Department, 557 Broadway, New York, NY 10012.

ISBN 978-0-545-56258-4

SCOOBY-DOO and all related characters and elements are trademarks of and © Hanna-Barbera.

Published by Scholastic Inc. All rights reserved.

SCHOLASTIC and associated logos are trademarks and/or registered trademarks of Scholastic Inc.

12 11 10 9 8 7 6 5 4 3 2 1   13 14 15 16 17 18/0

Designed by Rick DeMonico

Printed in the U.S.A.   40

First printing, August 2013

3 5444 00164256 9

CONTENTS

PROLOGUE

Lightning sliced through the sky over the Leroux Opera House. Thunder boomed and rain poured down. But inside the opera house, the staff of the television show *Talent Star* had no choice but to work through the storm—the show must always go on.

"Careful!" Dewey Ottoman, a balding, angry-faced man shouted at workers as they loaded scenery and TV equipment into the theater. "Lift with your legs! Your legs!" He shook his head, studying his clipboard. He looked up as someone walked past him with more set pieces. "Did you wipe your feet before you came in? I'm talking to you."

Dewey peered into a garbage can backstage. "Disgusting. The garbage in this trash can is filthy!" He turned to his assistant, Colette, whose main job was to follow him around. "You! I want this garbage cleaned at once! Hello!" He stormed to the center of the stage and yelled, "Is anyone listening to me? Am I the only one who cares about cleanliness?"

Suddenly, the enormous, glittering *Talent Star* sign that had been hanging high over Dewey's head crashed to the ground! It exploded in a shower of sparks, and the theater was plunged into darkness.

An eerie cackle rang out from above the stage. Everyone stared up into the theater's catwalks, where the sign had been hanging moments before. Sparks still rained down on the stage, illuminating a dark, cloaked figure, leaping from one catwalk to another. The figure grabbed a rope and swung down to the stage. He plucked Dewey's clipboard right out of his hands.

Dewey stared helplessly into the face of the figure. It was covered in a green half mask that looked like a skull. A moment later, the intruder swung away on his rope, still holding Dewey's clipboard. He made his escape through one of the theater's seating boxes. The only thing he left behind was the echo of his creepy laughter.

"The . . ." Dewey finally managed to croak out, "the . . . *the Phantom*!" He collapsed in center stage as the Phantom's cackling laughter rang out around him.

CHAPTER 1

Did you know Chicago is the third-largest city in the U.S.?" Velma sat under a teetering pile of travel books in the front seat of the Mystery Machine. She lifted her head to peek at Shaggy and Scooby beside her.

Shaggy clutched the van's steering wheel and licked his lips. "Like, I know Chicago has the best pizza!"

"Reah," Scooby said hungrily. "Rizza!"

Velma studied her book again. "Did you know Chicago has almost two hundred art galleries?"

Shaggy shook his head. "You really have no idea where my interests lie, do you?"

In the back of the van, Fred plucked at the strings of his guitar. Beside him, Daphne bounced with excitement. "I still can't believe Fred and I are really finalists on *Talent Star*! Have I mentioned it's my favorite show?"

Fred nodded. "Oh, once or twice."

". . . in *this breath*," Velma grumbled.

"Well, it is!" Daphne said. "And Brick Pimiento is the greatest host ever. Ooh, there he is!" She pointed to a huge billboard on the side of the road. The smiling face of Brick Pimiento, the host of *Talent Star*, stared down at them. "I really didn't think we were gonna make it through that last round of eliminations."

Fred grinned. "Come on, we had it sewn up! You know singers have the advantage." He started to play a new song on his guitar.

Shaggy leaned over the front seat to watch him. "Like, that's catchy!"

Fred looked up and gasped. "Keep your eyes on the road, Shaggy!"

"Right!" Shaggy said, turning back to focus on his driving.

"Wow, Fred," Daphne said. "That's beautiful. I really like you. It! I like *it*! Not you. I mean, I like you, but I don't . . . uh, I mean, I really like your song?"

"Thanks!" Fred grinned.

"You guys are good," Shaggy called from the driver's seat. "But me and Scooby are gonna beat you. Right, Scoob?"

"Reah!" Scooby bobbed his head.

Velma furrowed her eyebrows. "Uh, you're not in the competition."

"We will be once Brick sees our amazing juggling act!" Shaggy was absolutely convinced that he and Scooby were going to win *Talent Star*. There was just the small matter of getting themselves into the competition first.

"You can't just audition the day before the finals!" Fred protested.

"Like, you can if you're *awesome*!" Shaggy and Scooby high-fived.

Velma's attention was back on her guidebooks. "Okay," she said, pointing to a picture. "We definitely want to hit the Field Museum. . . . There's a Picasso exhibit at the Art Institute! Ooh! Ooh! The Mineralogical Society has the world-famous Soap Diamond on display!"

The rest of the gang stared at her blankly.

"Does it say anything in those books about that opera house where we're shooting the show?" Daphne wondered.

Velma paged through a book. "Yeah . . . the Leroux Opera House is almost a hundred years old. It's been closed since the seventies . . . and there are rumors that it's haunted."

Shaggy looked at Velma over a giant sandwich. "Of course it's haunted," he mumbled. "Like, when do we ever go to a place and it's *not* haunted?"

"Wait . . ." Velma said, looking first at the sandwich, then at Shaggy, who was suddenly in the seat right beside her. "Who's driving?"

Suddenly, Scooby yelled, "Reen means go!" He was thrilled to be driving the van. "Scooby-Dooby-Doo!"

Velma, Daphne, and Fred screamed. Shaggy munched happily on his sandwich as the Mystery Machine barreled down the road toward Chicago.

A few hours later, the gang pulled up outside the Leroux Opera House. "This place is amazing!" Velma said, staring at the ornate building. "I can't believe it's been closed for so long!"

As they approached the entrance, a security guard stopped Shaggy. "I'm sorry, sir. No animals allowed, except seeing-eye dogs."

"Fine," Shaggy said, turning to the others. "You guys go ahead. We'll catch up with you."

"Okay," Fred said, waving. "We'll see you later." He led the girls into the opera house.

Inside, the place was total chaos. Workers were dashing to and fro. Some of the show's other acts were milling around.

Daphne stopped one of the workers as he rushed through the lobby. "Hi," she said. "We're supposed to check in with the Assistant Director?"

"Dewey?" the guy asked. "Yeah, good luck with that. He's in there." He pointed to the auditorium.

On the stage, workers were cleaning up the remnants of the sign that had earlier fallen from the rafters. Dewey was slumped in a chair on stage left. Colette waved smelling salts under his nose, trying to wake him.

Suddenly, Dewey's eyes snapped wide open. "What . . . ? Where . . . ? What happened?"

"Uh," Colette said, "*you* know. That *guy*?"

Dewey's eyes widened. "The Phantom!" With a huge sigh, he passed out. Colette shrugged and waved the smelling salts under his nose again.

"Hello?" Daphne called. "We're supposed to check in."

"Yeah, I know," Colette said, sounding bored. "But you're gonna have to wait."

Dewey snapped awake again. "What . . . ?" he cried again. "Where . . . ? *The Phantom!*" His eyes fluttered, and he fainted.

Colette rolled her eyes. "He keeps doing that!" She pulled out another package of smelling salts.

"You know," Velma said, "overuse of smelling salts can damage the nasal passages."

"His or mine?" Colette asked.

"His."

Colette looked at Dewey, then shrugged again and poked the packet of salts under his nose.

Dewey startled awake for the third time. "THE PHANTOM!" Then he fainted again.

"The Phantom?" Fred asked.

A worker ran onto the stage. "Hey!" he called. "I found that clipboard the Phantom took!" He handed it to Colette. "Also, I quit. I ain't hangin' around this place for another second. It's haunted!"

The worker ran off. Colette stared down at the clipboard. Daphne, Velma, and Fred peered over her shoulder to see what it said.

"'Christine must win'?" Daphne said, pointing at the bright red words scrawled across the page.

"Guys . . ." Fred said. "It looks like we've got ourselves a mystery."

CHAPTER 2

"Chrissy does not give interviews unless she can approve all questions in advance!" Barb, a loud stage mother, shouted into her cell phone as she stormed into the theater. Chrissy, Barb's eight-year-old daughter, marched into the theater ahead of her.

"Backstage, Chrissy must be provided with a bowl of trail mix with everything but the peanuts removed!" Lance, Chrissy's father, screamed into *his* cell phone. "No! If I had meant a bowl of peanuts, I would have said a bowl of peanuts!"

"Chrissy will accept no questions regarding politics, religion, or her favorite color. Because I said so!" Barb barked into her phone.

"Well, hello there!" Daphne said to Chrissy. "Are you—?"

Barb and Lance immediately pushed themselves between Chrissy and Daphne.

"Are you trying to psych her out?" Lance
demanded.

"Is this some kind of weird mind game?"
Barb shrieked.

Daphne shrugged. "I was just saying hi—"

"Well, don't!" Lance ordered.

"You can't just *talk* to Chrissy!" said Barb.

"She's very sensitive!" Lance said, patting his
daughter's head.

Chrissy rolled her eyes, but her parents kept
talking.

"You have to talk to her before you talk to her
to let her know you're going to talk to her!" Lance
explained.

"Isn't that right, sweetie?!" Barb said.

Chrissy gave her parents a funny look.
"Whatever."

Barb and Lance both stared at Daphne
accusingly. "YOU SEE?!"

Barb went back to her phone while Lance
approached Colette. "We're here to check in,"

Lance told her, tapping his foot impatiently.

"We're checking in!" Barb screamed into her cell phone.

Colette looked at them for a moment. "Um, Mr. Ottoman's kind of unconscious right now?"

"Are you saying we can't check in?!" Lance gasped.

Barb looked as if this was the worst news she'd heard in years. She pressed her mouth to her phone and shouted, "THEY'RE SAYING WE CAN'T CHECK IN!"

"This is totally unacceptable," Lance spat out.

"Uh . . ." Colette was clearly at a loss for what to do.

"She said 'UH'!" Barb explained to the person on the other end of the phone.

Daphne, Fred, and Velma stood to the side, watching. That's when a sweet-faced twelve-year-old girl stepped over to them. "They're like that pretty much all the time," she whispered.

"Hey! You're Emma, right? The violinist?" Fred asked.

"Yeah," Emma said, shaking Fred's hand.

"And you're Fred Jones and Daphne Blake. I saw your audition tape. You guys were great. And I'm not just saying that because of the cameras."

"What cameras?" Velma asked, glancing around.

Emma pointed to the right, then up, and finally to the left. There were, in fact, cameras everywhere. "Those cameras," she said. "You know, they're catching all the backstage drama."

"That's the best part of the show," Daphne giggled. "All the 'who likes who, who hates who' stuff."

Emma nodded. "Just assume you're always on camera and don't do anything embarrassing."

"Helloooo, everyone!" Brick Pimiento swept onto the stage. He was grinning, but he also looked a little nervous. "Welcome to *Talent Star*! I'm your host, Brick Pimiento! I just want to reassure you all that everything is fantastic, just fantastic. There isn't a problem, nothing happened, and there's definitely no ghost."

Barb and Lance stared at him. "Ghost?!"

"Ghost?" Brick said, looking startled. "I didn't say ghost! Why would I say ghost when there's no ghost? Ha-ha-ha! Fantastic!" Brick laughed nervously.

Scooby and Shaggy had finally managed to sneak into the theater. They peeked out at the rest of the gang from their hiding place in the wings. "There he is!" Shaggy whispered, pointing to Brick.

"Reah!" Scooby barked.

On center stage, Brick stepped over to where Dewey sat slumped in the chair. "You're okay there, right, Dewey?" He rubbed Dewey's bald head, which squeaked like a balloon. Dewey didn't move, but Brick didn't seem to notice. "Ha-ha-ha! *Fantastic!* Well, carry on!" He hurried offstage.

Shaggy and Scooby tiptoed after Brick. As they crept past Dewey, he snapped awake. "I smell DOG!" Dewey blurted out, looking around. But Shaggy and Scooby were already long gone.

"Um," Colette said. "Mr. Ottoman, are you all ri—"

"Dogs are nothing but big furry sacks of germs!" Dewey hollered, suddenly alert again. "Did you know that?"

Colette looked puzzled. "I don't think—"

"I'm going to find that dog if it takes me all night!" Dewey grabbed his clipboard and stormed offstage.

Meanwhile, Shaggy and Scooby caught up to Brick Pimiento. "Mr. Pimiento!" Shaggy called. "Can we have, like, two minutes of your time? We've got an act that's just terrific!"

"Reah! Rerrific!" Scooby barked.

Brick grinned at them. "My friends, I've built my career on two deeply held beliefs. One, all talent deserves a chance to be seen. And two . . . juggling stinks. So, what have you got for me?"

Shaggy and Scooby froze. They looked at each other, and then looked down at the juggling balls in their hands. Shaggy hid the balls behind his back. He shrugged at Scooby, and a moment later they both started tap dancing. Unfortunately, neither of them knew *how* to tap dance.

Brick's smile slowly faded. It was clear that he'd rather be cleaning the garbage onstage than watching Scooby and Shaggy's clumsy dance moves.

Shaggy and Scooby tap-danced around a corner to get away. "Terrible," Shaggy moaned once they'd made their escape. "That was just—"

A scream cut off Shaggy before he could finish his sentence.

"Like, I don't know what that was," Shaggy said, shaking all over. "But I'm running away from it!"

"Re, roo!" Scooby cried.

CHAPTER 3

As the scream echoed through the theater, Brick Pimiento headed for the control room. Velma, Fred, and Daphne followed him into a room filled with television monitors. K.T., the *Talent Star* director, was frantically looking from screen to screen.

"Is it him?!" Brick asked.

"Yeah," K.T. pointed to one of the monitors. "It's the Phantom."

Everyone crowded in behind K.T. On-screen, they could see a cloaked figure with a white half mask standing in front of Chrissy. Chrissy screamed as Barb and Lance cowered behind her.

Velma pointed at the monitor. "There he goes!"

The Phantom ran out of the frame of the

monitor. Velma pointed as he appeared on another monitor. From the control room, they were able to watch him running through the halls of the theater. "Now he's there!" Velma exclaimed, as the Phantom dashed around a corner and reappeared on yet another monitor.

"We can track him this way!" Daphne cried.

Fred pulled out his cell phone. "Velma, you watch the monitors. You can tell me where he is." He began to run out of the room. "Daphne, you come with—"

"Yes!" said Daphne, following him.

A few minutes later, Fred put his phone to his ear. "Which way, Velma?"

"Right at the end of the hall!" Velma studied the monitors, watching as Fred and Daphne got closer and closer to the Phantom. "Second door on your left!"

Behind Velma, Brick looked at K.T. "Are you getting all this on camera?"

"Yeah!" K.T. grinned. "This is great stuff."

"Fantastic! Should we use it for promos, or leak it to WhoTube?"

"Both!" K.T. said.

As Velma watched, Fred and Daphne raced through the hallways of the opera house. They screeched to a halt in front of the second door on the left. Slowly, they opened the door. Fred reached inside and tried to turn on the light switch, but it didn't work. Using only the light from his cell phone, he and Daphne crept inside. A dark figure leaped out from behind a shelf and knocked over a rack of props as it fled the room.

"Look out!" Daphne yelped, pushing Fred out of the way.

"Are you okay?" Fred asked, standing up and straightening his ascot. Daphne nodded.

They hustled back out into the hall and looked around. "Which way?" Fred yelled into his phone.

"I don't know," Velma said, looking from monitor to monitor. "I can't see where he went!"

On the other side of the theater, Shaggy and Scooby slipped into the costume room. "He'll never think to look in here, right?"

"Right!" Scooby agreed, peeking out from behind a rack of clothes. He and Shaggy both sniffed at the air. "Ri smell remons."

"Yeah, I smell lemons, too," Shaggy agreed. He poked his nose out of the clothes rack and came face-to-face with a masked creature. "Do you smell lemons?" Shaggy asked the stranger. Then he realized it was the Phantom! *"Ahh!"*

"Ahh!" the Phantom screamed back.

Then all three of them ran out of the costume room.

In a hallway nearby, Fred and Daphne had no idea which way to go.

"There!" Velma said into her phone. She had finally spotted the Phantom again. "Go left! He's on the stairs!" As Velma watched, the Phantom looked directly at the camera . . . then dissolved away into nothingness. "What?!" she said, turning to Brick and K.T. "Did you see that?"

Brick and K.T. stared at the screen. Slowly, they both nodded.

Velma stared at the screen, perplexed. "Maybe he really *is* a ghost. . . ."

CHAPTER 4

A few minutes later, the gang assembled in the lobby. "How could the Phantom just disappear?" Daphne asked.

"There must be a rational explanation," Velma said.

"Yeah." Shaggy nodded. "Like he's a ghost."

"A ghost who smells like lemons?" Velma asked. "That sounds kinda weird."

Shaggy stared back at her. "And it's not weird to have a ghost who *doesn't* smell like lemons?"

Fred put his hands on his hips. "We have to get to the bottom of this."

Dewey marched into the lobby. "Dog!" he cried, pointing accusingly at Scooby.

Scooby looked around. "Rhere?"

"Get that germ sack out of here! *Right now!*" Dewey looked as if he was going to explode. "Did he leave footprints? I think I see footprints! He didn't touch any walls, did he? Ohmygosh, now I'll have to sanitize the entire building! Good thing I brought bleach." He pointed at Scooby again. "Out, I said! *Out out out!*"

Fred led the others toward the door. "Come on, guys."

As they walked out the front door of the opera house, they could hear Dewey yelling to Colette, "I want this carpet shampooed! And I want it *conditioned!*"

Outside, Velma took charge. "Okay, I'll check us into the hotel and do some Internet research. Shaggy and Scooby, you go to the library on State Street and see what you can find out about the opera house's history."

Shaggy looked at Scooby, then down at himself. "Like, how are *we* the choice for library research?"

Fred put one finger into the air. "I'll see what

I can find out here in the building. And, Daphne, you come with—"

"I'm going with Fred!" Daphne exclaimed.

A short while later, Velma stood in the lobby of the swanky Hotel Canard. "Welcome to the Hotel Canard. How may I be of service?" the hotel clerk greeted her.

Velma stepped up to the counter. "Hello, I need to check—*oof.*"

It was Barb. She'd shoved her way into the itty-bitty space between Velma and the check-in counter. "Hi! Checking in! Barb and Lance Damon! Oh, and Chrissy."

"I'm sorry," the clerk said, pointing at Velma. "But this young lady was—"

Lance squeezed in beside Barb. "Hey, are you giving us attitude?"

Barb huffed. "I think he's giving us attitude!"

"Buddy," Lance said in an unfriendly voice, "I want someone to take Chrissy's bags to the room *now*!" He pointed to a stack of luggage the size of a small bus.

The clerk looked at Velma helplessly.

"Go ahead," Velma muttered. "I'll wait." She stepped back to give Barb and Lance their space. "Oh, Chrissy!" Velma said, noticing Chrissy standing alone behind her. "Are you okay?"

Chrissy turned up her nose and rolled her eyes. "Of course I'm okay. Why wouldn't I be okay?"

"Weren't you scared of the Phantom?" Velma asked. "I mean, you were screaming, and—"

Chrissy laughed. "That wasn't a scared scream, silly. It was a happy scream, 'cause he told me I'm gonna win the competition."

"He told you—"

Chrissy cut Velma off. "I'm gonna win! Even if he has to obliterate all the other contestants. Isn't that *awesome*?"

Velma squinted at her. "Uh . . ."

"It's true!" said Barb. "We have a genuine psycho on our side! *Score!*"

26

Lance grinned. "That's why the Phantom wrote 'Christine must win' on that clipboard. Her name's Christine."

"But call her Chrissy," Barb cut in.

"Only, don't call her Chrissy, because don't talk to her at all," Lance said. "You're getting nerd breath all over her."

"Come on, Chrissy!" Barb said, pulling her daughter away. "Keep smiling."

As the Damons marched through the lobby, a magician strolled up beside Velma. "They're unbearable, aren't they?" he asked.

"Yeah, I . . ." Velma looked at him strangely. "Who are you?"

"I am . . . the Great Pauldini! My card." He held up an empty hand and, with a flourish, produced an egg.

"Uh, that's an egg."

The Great Pauldini looked annoyed. "Okay . . . egg, card, *whatever*. I made it appear, right? Can you do that? No, you can't. Because you're not a magician. Who's a magician?"

"You are?" Velma guessed.

"Oh, yeah," the Great Pauldini cheered. "Up high." He held up a hand to give Velma five, then sauntered off.

A voice beside Velma observed, "He's pretty unbearable himself."

Velma turned. There was no one there. "Hello?"

"Ahem." Velma looked down to find a three-foot-tall man standing beside her. "I'm Waldo," the man said. "The ventriloquist. And here's Hufnagel, my dummy." Waldo grabbed a six-foot-tall dummy off a luggage cart. "Hiya, toots!" he said, speaking in Hufnagel's voice. Velma shook her head, unimpressed.

As Waldo wandered off, four young girls strolled into the hotel lobby. "Hey," Velma said, pointing at them. "You guys are that band, right?"

"Yes! We are . . ." The four girls struck a pose, and then roared like dinosaurs. ". . . Girlasaurus Rex! *Roaaar!*"

One of the band members broke into a fit of giggles. "Ohmygosh, we are so *metal!*"

"Cathy . . ." Donna, another band member,

scowled at Cathy. "It's not metal to say 'Ohmygosh, we're so metal.'"

"Right," Cathy said, grinning. "Sorry." Cathy leaned in toward Velma to whisper, "We were a country act until three months ago."

Nancy, another girl in the band, growled. "We agreed we weren't telling people that! Now come on, look surly!"

As Girlasaurus Rex strode across the lobby, Velma rolled her eyes. "I think a lemon-scented ghost would fit right in with this crowd. . . ."

Back at the opera house, Fred and Daphne were searching for clues. "Fred?" Daphne said quietly. "Why do ghosts and monsters and stuff turn up wherever we go? Is it something about us?"

"No, this happens to everyone," said Fred, shrugging. "It would just be too much of a coincidence if this only happened to us. So logically, everyone must run into ghosts and monsters all the time."

"Really?" Daphne looked amazed.

"It's simple math," Fred said confidently. "They must be everywhere." He opened a door leading off the hallway, and then jumped back. A nervous, middle-aged man was hiding in the dark.

"*Ahh!*" Fred and Daphne cried.

"What are you doing in here?" the man demanded.

"What are *you* doing in here?" Fred asked, opening the door wider.

"I'm Mel Richmond," the man explained. "I own this building and I have a right to lurk in it." Mel studied Daphne and Fred. "You must be from the show, right?"

Fred puffed up his chest. "We're contestants."

"Right," Mel said. "Well, good luck to you."

"Mr. Richmond," Fred asked. "Do you know anything about the Phantom?"

"Ugh . . . that business again. Look, that was all way before my time. I inherited this place a few years ago when my father passed away." Mel shrugged.

"I'm so sorry," Daphne said.

"Me, too," Mel agreed. "It's costing me thousands of dollars a week. I can't do *anything* with it. People are still spooked by that Phantom nonsense, and that was thirty-five years ago!"

"*What* was thirty-five years ago?" prompted Fred.

Mel sighed. "It happened back in the seventies. Before that, there had been some . . . oddities at the Leroux Opera House. But nothing scary." Mel sighed again. "The trouble started when my father turned the place into a disco."

Fred and Daphne leaned in closer as Mel continued his story. "The Phantom wreaked havoc every night. But he was never seen without his mask. They say the mask hid a face of such terrible deformity that to gaze upon it would drive a man mad! No one was ever badly hurt, but the Phantom terrorized the clubgoers, he destroyed the sound system, he set fires. . . ."

Mel paused. "Finally, my father just had to close the place down. This place has been a money pit ever since—all because of that ridiculous Phantom. I wasn't able to rent it at all until the *Talent Star* people came around." Mel kicked at a piece of scenery. "Now they say the Phantom's back! Well, maybe I'll get lucky and he'll burn the place down so I can collect the insurance money, eh? Or maybe I should put on a cape and a mask and do it myself!"

Mel laughed, but stopped when he saw the way Daphne and Fred were looking at him. He shrugged. "What? Aw, now, don't look at me like that! You see, that's why I don't make jokes."

CHAPTER 5

"**Y**ou know what I like best about going to the library, Scoob?" Shaggy looked over at his best pal as they walked down a dark Chicago street.

"Rhe rooks?"

"No, the fact that's it's far, far away from that Phantom guy."

Scooby nodded. "Reah."

"And it's nice that Velma trusts us with an important assignment like—" Suddenly, a delicious aroma caught Shaggy's attention. He and Scooby both stopped and sniffed the air. "PIZZA!"

The two friends turned and raced toward the smell—in the opposite direction of the library. "Gimme eat!" Shaggy gasped as they barged into Giovanni's Pizzeria.

"Right this way, sir." A waitress led Shaggy and Scooby toward a round table.

Shaggy and Scooby looked over the menu hungrily. "Do you, like, have anything bigger than the extra extra large?" Shaggy asked.

"Yeah . . . but it's not on the menu, and you have to sign a release saying we're not responsible if you die." The waitress studied them.

Shaggy and Scooby grinned at each other. "We'll take it," Shaggy announced.

"All righty. Uh, but I'm gonna have to move you to another table."

"Why?"

The waitress pointed at their table, which could easily fit five or six people. "Because this one's smaller than your pizza."

Shaggy and Scooby beamed. *"Awwwwesome!"*

A few minutes later, several waiters wheeled out a cart carrying an enormous, six-foot-long pizza.

"Like, I've dreamed of this moment all my life, Scoob." Shaggy licked his lips.

"Re, roo!"

"Only in my dream, I'm in my pajamas and the pizza is served by talking sea monkeys."

"Re, roo!"

The waiters slid the pizza onto Shaggy and Scooby's table. The waitress returned to check on them. "We can wrap up the leftovers for you," she offered.

Shaggy and Scooby both burst out laughing. "Left . . . *overs*? Leftovers! That's hilarious!" They tore into the pizza.

Just as Shaggy and Scooby were popping the last slices into their mouths, the door of Giovanni's burst open and a woman wearing huge sunglasses and head-to-toe sparkles entered. Everyone in the restaurant began taking pictures.

"Roo's rat?" asked Scooby, licking his paws.

"Like, that's Lotte!" Shaggy said. "She's on *Talent Star*, but she's already won a bunch of other talent shows."

The waitress leaned over their table to whisper, "She was great on *America's Got Singing* and *Sing or Die* and *Singetty-Sing-Sing*!"

A big guy pushed a piece of paper in front of

35

Thompson Nicola Regional District Library System

Lotte. "Can you sign this? It's for my niece. Her name's Bob."

Lotte signed it, and then she moved to the next table, where some guy wanted her to sign his tongue.

A girl wearing shorts and tights ran up to Lotte with an autograph book. Lotte looked her up and down. "Uh-uh. I do not sign for anyone wearing tights and shorts. Because it's *wrong!*" The girl burst into tears and hurried away. "Yeah, you better run!" Lotte called after her.

Lotte headed straight for Shaggy and Scooby's table. "Leave us," she told the waitress.

The waitress did as she was told.

Lotte stabbed a long, razor-sharp fingernail into the tabletop in front of Shaggy and Scooby. "I want you to take a message to Daphne and Fred," she hissed. "Tell them they don't stand a chance." She narrowed her eyes. "I will crush all who oppose me. I will feast upon their blood! I will make their families weep! I will *leave nothing but their scarves!*" She threw the table aside and picked up Shaggy by his shirt. "So swears Lotte!"

She slashed the letters of her name into Shaggy's shirt with her fingernail. *"L-o-t-t-e!"*

Shaggy and Scooby both leaped up from the table and ran screaming into the night, leaving nothing but a streak of pizza sauce behind them.

CHAPTER 6

"Hey, guys!" Shaggy ran into the gang's hotel suite. He was out of breath and panting, like a dog after a nice long run.

"Where have you two been?" Velma asked. "The library closed hours ago!"

Shaggy gave her a funny look. "The what?"

"Never mind." Velma sighed. "I found plenty of information online. There was definitely a Phantom back in the seventies." She showed the rest of the gang a blurry old picture on her laptop. "But I don't think the one we saw today was the same person." She pointed at a second picture on her computer screen. "This picture is from earlier tonight."

"Where did you get that?" Daphne asked.

"It's all over the Internet," Velma explained.

"*Talent Star* is really milking this whole Phantom thing for publicity." She pointed at the two pictures again. The Phantom in the second picture had a slightly different outfit than the first, and the mask was a different shape. "See? The outfit is different. I think what we saw today was someone taking advantage of the old stories for their own purposes."

"But you saw him disappear, right?" Daphne argued. "He must be a real ghost!"

Velma rolled her eyes. "I saw it *on a monitor.* It could have been faked."

"So who are the likely suspects?" Fred asked.

"Definitely Chrissy's parents," Daphne said.

"Yeah," Fred agreed. "The Phantom seems awfully interested in making sure Chrissy wins the competition."

Velma typed in "Barb and Lance." Then she added, "And Brick Pimiento. He was a little too quick to capitalize on the Phantom for publicity. . . . Could he be doing this to boost the show's ratings?"

Fred nodded. "Mel Richmond, the guy who

owns the opera house." He looked at Daphne. "Maybe what he said about insurance money wasn't such a joke."

"What about Dewey Ottoman?" said Daphne. "He's creepy."

"Does he have a motive?" Fred asked.

"Isn't *creepy* a motive?" Daphne shuddered.

Velma typed in "Dewey Ottoman."

"Ooh! Ooh! You've gotta put Lotte down!" said Shaggy.

"You think Lotte is the Phantom?" Daphne asked.

"I think she's scarier than the Phantom," Shaggy said. "Put her down."

Velma typed in *Lotte*. "*Hmm* . . . everyone on this list, except Mel Richmond and Lotte, has been seen at the same time as the Phantom."

Fred stretched and yawned. "Guys, it's getting late. We have the dress rehearsal in the morning, and then the big show tomorrow night. I say we get some sleep."

About an hour later, as almost everyone in the hotel slept, a dark figure slipped through the halls of the Hotel Canard.

Inside the gang's suite, Shaggy rolled over. "Scooby-Doo? I can't sleep."

"Re reither," Scooby whispered. "Roo ront the bed?" Scooby sat up in bed and looked down at Shaggy, who was curled up on the floor.

"No," Shaggy said, stretching. "It's been almost two hours since that pizza, and I'm starving! Maybe the hotel has a vending machine or something."

Quietly, Shaggy and Scooby opened the door of the suite. Shaggy pulled the door closed behind him, then turned and came face-to-face with a dark figure sneaking out of Lotte's room across the hall. It was the Phantom! He was holding a small spray bottle in his hand, and he didn't look too happy to see them.

"*Ahh!*" Shaggy cried, turning to pound on the door to their suite. "Let us in!" He jiggled the doorknob, but it was locked. The Phantom drew closer, laughing.

Shaggy and Scooby turned and bolted. Careening down the hall, the two friends crashed into Dewey Ottoman.

"Dog!" Dewey screamed, obviously much more concerned about Scooby than about the Phantom zipping down the hall behind him. "I touched a dog! I have dog bacteria!"

Shaggy and Scooby ran on. They zigzagged through the hotel's halls and finally plowed through a set of doors into a banquet room. Panting, they searched for an exit—but couldn't find one.

A moment later, the Phantom ran in and slammed the doors closed. Shaggy and Scooby backed away in fear.

The Phantom merely laughed, then pushed over a huge cabinet in front of the doors, blocking the only way out.

"Like, take it easy there, guy. . . ." Shaggy begged.

"Reah . . ." Scooby said, nodding.

The Phantom reached into a busboy station and pulled out a large knife. He laughed as he crept toward Scooby and Shaggy.

Shaggy jumped back. "That's not taking it easy! That's taking it very, very hard!"

Outside, someone began to pound on the doors. But the toppled cabinet made it impossible for them to get in! Shaggy and Scooby looked around desperately as the Phantom drew closer and closer.

Finally, Scooby spotted a door on the other side of the room. "Rhere!"

Scooby and Shaggy escaped onto a patio filled with tables. The Phantom followed them, waving his knife menacingly. Scooby and Shaggy backed away from him until they were pressed up against a railing and could go no farther. *"Ahhhh!"*

The Phantom's knife glinted in the moonlight. Just when he was close enough to reach out and touch them, a net dropped down on top of him. He was trapped!

"Hah!" Fred said happily. Daphne and Velma ran out to the patio, followed by Brick, Dewey, Waldo, and Lotte.

The Phantom just laughed. Suddenly, a puff of smoke filled the air. When it cleared, the Phantom was nowhere to be seen. He had disappeared!

"It's been cut," Fred said, picking up the empty net.

Brick held out his hands to try to calm everyone. "It's okay, everyone. He's gone. No harm done. Everybody back to bed. Fantastic."

As they started back into the hotel, Shaggy and Scooby bumped into Lotte. *"Ahh!"* they screamed.

"Enough with the screaming," Lotte groaned. "Yeesh." She pointed at Fred and Daphne. "Gonna skin you alive. G'night."

"Hey," Shaggy said, sniffing the air. "No lemons."

"Reah," Scooby-Doo agreed. "Rou're right."

Velma and Daphne joined Fred, who was still studying his net. "That smoke bomb seemed like something a magician would do," Velma observed. "And the Great Pauldini's nowhere to be seen."

Fred nodded. "True. But does he have a motive?"

Daphne shrugged. "This just keeps getting more mysterious."

44

"You know what the real mystery is?" Velma asked, turning to Fred. "How did you get hold of a net in the middle of the night?"

"Uh, well, I . . ." Fred blushed.

"Ohmygosh!" Velma gasped. "You sleep with a net, don't you?!"

Fred shrugged. "Lots of people do!"

CHAPTER 7

The next morning, the *Talent Star* performers made their way back to the Leroux Opera House for a dress rehearsal. Daphne, Fred, and Velma entered the lobby first, followed by Shaggy, who was dressed as a mom pushing a baby carriage.

A security guard bent down to look in the stroller. "Aww, look at the little . . ." He paused, then gave Shaggy a funny look. ". . . baby?"

Scooby-Doo, who was holding a rattle and wearing a bonnet, said, "Gooby-gooby-goo?"

The guard looked confused, but Shaggy just pushed past him and rolled Scooby inside.

Onstage, carpenters were bustling around, trying to finish the glitzy, glittery set. The giant

Talent Star sign was fixed and back in its place above the stage.

"Okay, people," Dewey shouted, glancing down at his clipboard. "We've only got one dress rehearsal, so let's get it right. Chrissy Damon, you're up first!"

In the wings, Chrissy screamed, "If I want two idiots barking at me, I'll hire a pair of pugs!"

Lance shouted over her, "I told you three times to grease her teeth and are they greased? No!"

Barb ignored them both. "She needs at least another half pound of glitter in her hair!"

"Chrissy!" Dewey yelled, trying to get their attention.

Chrissy snapped to attention and fixed her face into a sweet little smile. "Ready!" She skipped onto the stage and performed her song beautifully.

"Next is . . . Emma Gale." Dewey studied the microphone. "Has anyone cleaned this microphone recently?"

"Like, an hour ago?" Colette said.

"Unbelievable!" Dewey shrieked. "What are

we, savages?" He spritzed the microphone with cleanser and wiped it off.

Emma made her way to the stage, holding a violin. But not just any violin—an electric violin!

"Ohmygosh, she is so amazing!" Daphne exclaimed as Emma played. Daphne turned to two people watching from the wings. "Are you Emma's parents?"

"Mike and Meg Gale," Mike said, nodding. "Pleased to meet you! Isn't she terrific?"

"Yeah," Fred agreed. "I think she's got a good shot at winning."

Meg grinned. "We sure hope so. Without that prize money, the bank's going to take our farm."

"Oh!" Fred gasped. "That's . . . terrible."

"Yeah, it's been in our family for five generations," Meg explained. "Mike's grandparents are buried there."

"So . . ." Mike said, changing the subject. "What are you two going to do with the money if you win?"

Daphne turned red. "Uh . . . just thinking, maybe . . ."

"We could, uh, use some new, um, seat covers for the van. . . ." Fred said.

"Um, possibly a hat?" Daphne added with a nervous shrug. The Gales smiled politely.

As soon as Emma finished playing, Dewey announced, "Next up—Lotte Lavoie!"

Backstage, Lotte scolded her assistants as they finished her hair and makeup. "Now, throat spray!" One of Lotte's assistants handed her a spray bottle, and Lotte sprayed a special tonic on her vocal chords. Then she swept out onto the stage and began her song. But in place of her beautiful voice, there was a horrible, painful squawk—she sounded like a dying crow.

Lotte stopped singing and pressed her hand to her throat. Everyone in the wings stopped talking and stared at her. "*Crooooooak!*" She cleared her throat. "Who did this to me? *Who?!*" Her voice was crackly and rough, as if someone had sprinkled pebbles down her throat. "Someone is going to pay for this! *Someone is going to pay!*"

The *Talent Star* staff ushered Lotte backstage. A doctor sat her down to look at her throat.

"Her throat has been sprayed with some kind of chemical irritant," he explained. "There's no permanent damage, but you won't be able to sing for at least a week."

"I'm gonna sue you!" Lotte hissed in her scary voice. "And you! And you! And *everyone*!" She pointed wildly around at the groups of people who had gathered in the wings. She stormed off. "SOMEONE HAD BETTER FIX THIS OR I'M GOING TO GET MAD!"

"So . . . do you think the Phantom is behind this?" Daphne asked Fred.

"Could be," Fred said.

Dewey, who didn't seem particularly concerned, barreled on. "We're behind schedule, people! Next up are . . . Blake and Jones!"

"We'll keep an eye open for the Phantom," Velma promised as Daphne and Fred made their way toward the stage.

As they began to sing, Scooby spotted the silhouette of a caped figure in the shadows backstage. Scooby nudged Shaggy, and they hustled over to check it out.

The two buddies climbed up to a catwalk that stretched over the stage. Below, the figure moved into the light and they could see that it was Brick Pimiento, with his coat slung over his shoulder. He'd only *looked* like the Phantom.

"Like, it's only Brick—" Shaggy said. Then he swung his arms around, trying to catch his balance.

Too late! The catwalk tipped, and Shaggy and Scooby fell, hurtling toward the stage below. They landed directly on top of Brick.

"Sorry, sir!" Shaggy cried, helping Brick to his feet. "Sorry!"

"Was that your new act?" Brick asked, brushing himself off. "What are you, the human cannonball?"

"No, we thought you were the Phantom!" Shaggy explained.

Brick laughed nervously. "Why would you think that? That's crazy!"

Scooby and Shaggy shrugged as Brick hurried away.

Onstage, Daphne and Fred had just finished

singing. "Next! The Great Pauldini!" announced Dewey.

The Great Pauldini hopped onstage in his top hat and tails. He spread his arms wide as a curtain dropped around him. The moment the bottom of the curtain reached the floor, it disappeared—to reveal he'd vanished!

In the wings, the gang applauded, impressed.

"Still no sign of the Phantom," Velma mused.

"Maybe the whole thing's over," Daphne said.

Dewey's voice cut off their conversation. "Waldo and Hufnagel!"

Waldo stepped onto the stage with his giant dummy. "Say, Hufnagel, are you an actor or a dummy?"

"What's the difference?" Hufnagel replied.

In the wings, the members of Girlasaurus Rex looked on. "Ohmygosh, he's on fire!" Cathy cried, pointing at the stage. Waldo's dummy had caught fire.

"Hufnagel," Waldo asked his dummy. "Do you . . . smell something burning?!" The fire raced up the dummy's leg.

Velma rushed onto the stage with a fire extinguisher just as the Phantom's voice rang out from above them: "Christine must win!"

Waldo stormed off the stage, dragging a dripping, charred Hufnagel behind him. Brick caught him as he ran away. "Waldo? Hey, you're not leaving are you, buddy?"

"No," Waldo said, staring back at Brick. "I thought I'd stay and risk my life for a stupid talent show."

Brick grinned. "That's fantastic! I—"

"Of course I'm leaving!" Waldo screamed. He turned to look at the other performers gathering around them. "And the rest of you will leave, too, if you have any sense!"

Waldo rushed out of the theater. Before the doors closed behind him, Dewey was back at his microphone. "Girlasaurus Rex! You're on!"

The girls in the band rushed to the stage. Cathy took center stage. "We are . . ."

"Girlasaurus Rex!" the band yelled together. They all roared.

"One, two, one-two-three-four!" Nancy called

out into the microphone. The band was ready to rock—but the moment they began to play, their instruments fell apart. The drums collapsed into useless piles of metal, their guitar strings broke, and the neck of the bass guitar broke off.

The girls in the band all stared at one another helplessly. Then the Phantom's voice cried out, "Christine must win!" His eerie laughter echoed through the theater again.

Dewey looked frantic. "K.T.! Where is he? *Where is the Phantom?*"

K.T., who'd been watching the action from the control room, answered through his headset. "He's in the prop room!" As K.T. watched, the Phantom disappeared, and then reappeared in another room. "No, wait! He's in the coffee—" K.T.'s jaw dropped as the Phantom disappeared and then reappeared again and again. Every time he reappeared, he was in a different room. "He's in . . . he's everywhere! What the heck?"

"Find him! Now!" Dewey yelped.

Nancy and the other members of Girlasaurus

Rex tossed their broken instruments into a heap on the stage.

"Right," Nancy said hastily. "We're outta here."

Brick Pimiento chased them as they strode toward the exit. "Where are you going? Come on!"

"Dude," Donna said, "someone busted our instruments. What's next, our heads?"

Meanwhile, Fred gathered Daphne, Velma, Shaggy, and Scooby together. "We've got to do something. Velma, you've seen all the acts, right?"

"Yeah," Velma said slowly.

"Who do you think the frontrunners are? I mean, of the ones that are left?"

"Honestly? You guys, the violin girl, and Chrissy."

Daphne said, "So if the Phantom wants Chrissy to win, he'll try to get rid of Emma and us."

Fred nodded. "Velma, can you get Emma's parents to take her someplace safe?"

"Sure."

"We're going to set a trap for the Phantom," Fred said, turning to Daphne. "And, Daphne, we'll be the bait."

CHAPTER
8

Well, we're gonna go take a nap now!" Fred announced a few minutes later, strolling onto center stage.

A stagehand looked at him as if he was crazy. "Um, no one cares?"

"Yep!" Fred chirped. "So we'll be asleep and napping! Totally unprotected!"

"Yes, in our dressing room," Daphne added. "Asleep!"

Fred called out, "Unguarded! Here we go!"

They headed for their dressing room. Velma, Shaggy, and Scooby waited in their closet, hiding among the costumes.

"Hang tight," Fred whispered to the gang. "Something's bound to happen."

"To you, right?" Shaggy whispered back. "Not

to us?" Velma glared at him. "What?" Shaggy demanded. "I'm just asking."

"Rit's a rair ruestion," Scooby said, nodding.

Minutes passed. "Just a matter of time now," Daphne whispered. She and Fred each laid down on a couch and pretended to sleep.

More minutes passed, then hours.

"This is ridiculous," Shaggy muttered. "We've been waiting forever!" He turned to where Velma had been standing beside him. "And, Velma, would you get your elbow out of my ribs?"

"I'm over here, Shaggy," Velma hissed from the other side of the closet.

"Then whose elbow . . . ?" Shaggy peered into the darkness and came face-to-face with the Phantom. He screamed. The Phantom screamed back.

The closet door flew open and Shaggy, Scooby, and Velma all toppled out.

"What is it?" asked Fred, sitting up.

"Ph-ph-ph-Phantom!" Shaggy stuttered.

Fred hurried to the closet and shoved the clothes aside. "He must have gone through here."

Fred pointed to a hidden door in the back of the closet. He climbed through the door, gesturing for the others to follow.

"Like, I hate hidden passages!" said Shaggy as they crept down a dark, narrow passageway. "They never lead anywhere good. When's the last time we were in a hidden passage and it led to, like, miniature golf?"

A few minutes later, the passageway grew wider. "We're in the sewer below the opera house!" Velma said.

"But, like, how are we gonna find—" Shaggy gulped.

"*Shhh!*" Daphne said. She pointed. Faint organ music was playing in the distance. Daphne led the others past dripping pipes and tunnels full of rats, listening for the music. "There it is again!"

Scooby-Doo pointed with his ears. "Ris ray!"

The gang followed Scooby into a cavernous tunnel filled with furniture and candles. The Phantom was sitting in front of a huge pipe organ. "Aha!" he said, turning to face them. "I suppose it was only a matter of time until someone found

The kids from Mystery, Inc. are participating in the *Talent Star* reality TV competition.

But—ruh-roh!—a spooky Phantom is haunting the opera house!

The Phantom is determined to stop anyone who gets in his way.

Fred and Daphne interview the suspects, including the opera house's owner...

...while Velma has her own ideas about who's behind the Phantom's mask.

The show's assistant director, Dewey, is definitely involved.

Another case closed for the kids from Mystery, Inc.!

me. Welcome to my home!" He gestured to the creepy cave. "I have lived here in the dank, reeking sewers all my life, forced to hide from society to conceal the hideous, twisted mass of flesh that is my face! But now, I can hide no longer!"

The Phantom whipped off his mask. "Behold, the Phantom of the Opera!"

The gang all stared in shocked silence. Finally, Daphne muttered, "Um . . . you look fine?"

"I . . . what?" the Phantom demanded.

"I mean, you're no Brad Pitt or anything, but you're okay," Daphne said, staring at him.

The Phantom rushed over to an ornate mirror surrounded by candles. "But look! Gaze upon my foul, deformed visage! I'm hideous! *Hideous!*"

Shaggy walked up behind him. "Dude, this is a funhouse mirror."

The Phantom looked surprised. "I . . . it is? But this is the only mirror I've ever looked in. I mean, I don't have any others, and when I go out I always wear the mask."

Daphne held up her pocket mirror, and the Phantom gazed at himself. "Hey!" He gasped. "I look *good!*" He chuckled uneasily. "Well, this is embarrassing. Wow, I really wish I had the last thirty-five years back. Uh . . . so it's . . . super-awkward right now. I, uh . . . yeah."

"Mr. Phantom?" Fred said.

"Steve," the Phantom said. "Steve Trilby."

"Steve, why have you been sabotaging the talent show?" Fred asked.

"The what now?"

"Talent Star?" Daphne prompted. "The TV show? You wrecked some instruments and set fire to a dummy, and—"

"Not me," Steve blurted out. "I haven't been up above at all lately, except to get food."

"Is that why you were in our dressing room?" Fred wondered.

"Yeah," Steve said, shrugging. "That's the secret door closest to the vending machines. I like those little burritos? The bean-and-cheese ones?"

"But," Velma said, "back in the seventies . . ."

Steve looked embarrassed. "Oh, uh, yeah. Well . . . yeah, I did some stuff back then. Stuff I'm not proud of." He looked annoyed. "It was when they turned the opera house into a disco! I loved the opera so much. I can hear everything from down here, you know. But that disco music just made me crazy! Anyway, that was when I was young and impetuous. I haven't bothered anyone for almost thirty-five years now."

He turned to Daphne. "Could I, uh . . . could I see that mirror again?" Daphne passed him the mirror. "Look at me! I'm an Adonis!"

As Steve gazed at his reflection, Velma pulled the others aside. "Guys, I'm pretty sure he's telling the truth."

"But if he isn't behind everything that's been going on," Fred wondered, "then who—?"

Before Fred could finish his thought, a scream rang out from above them. The Phantom had struck again!

CHAPTER 9

The gang raced through the dank tunnels and back up to the opera house. It was almost pitch-black in the auditorium. On center stage, Colette was screaming in terror. When they looked up, they saw the Great Pauldini dangling high above her head. Fred rushed to turn the lights on. Once the stage was lit up, the gang realized the Great Pauldini was hanging from a harness. He appeared to be fine.

"Hey!" the magician called down. "Uh, kinda stuck up here."

"Oh!" Colette exclaimed when she realized he was okay. She shrugged and walked offstage.

"So, could someone get a ladder, or . . . ?" The Great Pauldini waved his arms in midair.

"What happened?" Velma yelled up to him.

"The harness is part of my disappearing trick," the magician explained. "I was working on it when the Phantom shoved me off a catwalk!"

Steve, who'd followed the gang out of his hidden lair, suddenly pointed into darkness over the stage. "Look!"

The Phantom was dashing across the catwalks above them, setting fire to the curtains with a blowtorch.

"I'm going after him!" Fred called.

"We'll put out that fire!" Shaggy offered.

When he realized he'd been spotted, the Phantom bolted across one catwalk and scurried up another. Fred climbed after him. Just as Fred reached out to unmask the Phantom, the creep fired up his blowtorch and pointed it right at Fred!

"Look out!" Daphne yelled.

Fred bent backward, dodging the Phantom's fire. He grabbed the Phantom by the wrist, but the Phantom squirmed out of his grasp. Fred could feel the fire getting closer to his face when Steve zipped by on a rope and knocked the Phantom off the catwalk. Both Steve and the Phantom fell to a lower catwalk, and then tumbled the remaining ten feet to the stage below them.

"I think . . . I'm dying. . . ." Steve gasped, as Velma raced to trap the Phantom.

Daphne looked at him. "Um, actually, I'm pretty sure you're okay."

Steve pointed at his face in the mirror. "But look, I'm all bloody!"

"There's just some red paint on the . . . do you understand how mirrors work *at all*?" Daphne asked.

Steve sat up. "Gimme a break, I grew up in a sewer!"

On the other side of the stage, Velma had the Phantom secured. She reached down and pulled off his mask. "Mel Richmond!" she exclaimed, gaping at the theater owner.

"So you *were* going to burn the place down for the insurance money!" Fred exclaimed.

"Yes!" Mel spat. "And I would have gotten

away with it, too, if it hadn't been for you meddling kids and your nosy dog!"

"Dog?" A security guard perked up. "Where?!"

"Zoinks!" Shaggy yelped.

"Ruh-roh!" Shaggy and Scooby ran off, with the security guard in hot pursuit.

Dewey Ottoman walked onstage with a pair of police officers.

"Is this the guy?" One of the police officers pointed at Mel.

"That's him, Officer," Dewey nodded. "Mel Richmond."

As the police started to lead Mel away, Velma stopped them. "Wait! This still doesn't make sense."

"If you wanted the insurance money, why didn't you just burn the place down? Why do all that other stuff?" Daphne asked.

"I didn't!" Mel said, shrugging. "But whoever did gave me the idea to put on this costume. Stupidest idea I ever had . . ."

As Mel muttered to himself, an eerie cackle rang out of the sound system. "Ha-ha-ha! Christine must win!"

"Huh? Wha? What the heck?" The policeman looked stumped.

"Otherwise, I will rain death and destruction down upon this place!" the creepy voice cried. "So swears the Phantom! Ha-ha-ha!"

The officers jumped to the side as a huge light fixture crashed down right next to them.

"Now will you take this seriously?" Dewey demanded. "I want as many officers as you can spare here for the show tonight!"

"I was thinking the same thing, buddy." The policeman looked worried. "We're on it."

Dewey rushed after the officers as they led Mel away. Fred, Daphne, and Velma trailed behind them. "So you'll do it?" Dewey begged. "You'll put all your men on this?"

"Hello?" the Great Pauldini called out as the others left the stage. "I still need a ladder! Hey! *The Great Pauldini is not pleased!*"

Out in the hall, Shaggy and Scooby were fleeing from the security guard.

"Stop that dog!" The guard chased them down the hallway, but Shaggy and Scooby jumped up and clung to a hanging light on the hallway ceiling as the guard ran past.

Brick Pimiento peeked out of the sound-room door just below Shaggy and Scooby.

"Brick!" Shaggy called, flopping to the floor.

"Ahh!" Brick screamed, startled. "I wasn't doing anything . . . I was just in there! Not doing anything! I mean, I was doing something, but it was nothing!"

"Like, we have a totally great act for you!" said Shaggy, unruffled by Brick's odd behavior.

"Oh!" Brick grinned. "Oh. Well, fantastic! By all means, proceed!"

"Say, Scooby?" Shaggy began. "What bone will a dog never eat?"

Scooby giggled. "Ri ron't know, Raggy!"

"A *trom*bone!"

Brick stared at Shaggy. "Um, yeah, that's fan—" He broke off, then yelled, *"Security!"*

As Shaggy and Scooby backed away, they tried one last joke.

"Say, Scooby . . . what vegetable do you get when you cross a dog with a rose?"

"Ri ron't know, Raggy!"

"A COLLIE-FLOWER!" Shaggy dashed around the corner just as a security guard appeared.

"Dog!" the security guard called. He chased them down the hall.

Brick turned to greet Velma, Daphne, and Fred, who were approaching from the other direction. "Blake and Jones! Well, you must be happy!"

"Why?" Daphne asked.

"Your odds of winning are way up. There are only four acts left!"

"Three," Velma muttered. "The Great Pauldini just quit." She watched, eyes narrowed, as Brick carefully pulled the door to the sound room closed behind him.

"Whatever," Brick said. "Anyway, the publicity the Phantom has generated has been *fantastic*! We're expecting our highest ratings ever!" He led Daphne and Fred down the hall. "Come on, let me

68

show you the latest viewer projections."

Velma waited until they were out of sight, then opened the door to the sound room. "The sound room, huh?" She poked around, noticing a microphone set up on a table stand. "It's still on." She traced the microphone's wire and saw that it was plugged into a jack labeled STAGE. "So anything said into this microphone would be heard onstage. Interesting . . ."

She hurried down the hall to the control room, where K.T. was preparing for that night's show. "Do you keep the footage all the cameras in here shoot?" she asked.

K.T. nodded. "Well, sure. There's a whole digital database on the server."

"Could I look through it?"

"Sure. But there's, like, two thousand hours of footage in there."

"Oh, man!" Velma said, pulling out the brochure for the Mineralogical Society. "Now there's no way I'm gonna have time to see the Soap Diamond."

CHAPTER 10

Later that night, a huge crowd was going wild outside the opera house. The live coverage of *Talent Star* was about to start, and the whole street around the theater was jam-packed. The outside of the building was lit up with roving spotlights. Crowds of reporters held their cameras high, taking shot after shot. Police swarmed over everything.

"*Talent Star* was starting to get kind of old," a woman in the crowd shouted to her friend. "But this Phantom thing has really spiced it up!"

Inside the theater, the houselights went down and the stage lit up. Everyone applauded as the *Talent Star* theme music started.

"Ladies and gentlemen! Welcome to the *Talent Star* finals!" Brick Pimiento grinned in the spotlight at center stage. "I'm your host, Brick Pimiento!" He tried to tuck his grin away as he added, "Now, I'm sure all of you have heard that we've had some . . . trouble."

A large screen flashed on, showing video clips of the Phantom at work. "Terrible business," Brick said. "Because of this so-called 'Phantom,' we're down to just three acts. Emma, Blake and Jones, and Chrissy. By the end of the show tonight, one will be crowned this year's Talent Star!"

Everyone in the audience whooped. They fell silent again as a giant box of Fudge-A-Roni was rolled onto the stage. Brick gestured to it. "The others will receive a year's supply of Fudge-A-Roni: the great taste of fudge, with the convenience of 'roni!"

From the wings, Shaggy and Scooby—now dressed as an old man to thwart the security guards—were drooling.

"As you know, on *Talent Star*," Brick continued, "*you* decide the winner! Your votes will be tallied in real time and displayed on this scoreboard." Numbers flashed across the scoreboard.

"And now, going out live all over the world, I give you . . . Chrissy!"

As Chrissy took the stage, Emma was back in her dressing room, preparing. While she was busy fixing her hair, a gloved hand reached out of the shadows and grabbed her violin.

An instant later, Fred reached out and grabbed the gloved hand. "You were right, Emma!" Fred cried, coming face-to-face with the Phantom. "You *do* make better bait than us!"

The Phantom elbowed Fred and dashed out of Emma's dressing room—straight into Scooby and Shaggy!

"*Oof!*" The three of them bounced off one another, landing in a heap in the hall. Scooby's wig and beard were askew.

Daphne and Fred rushed out of Emma's dressing room and pulled off the Phantom's mask.

"Lance Damon!" Daphne announced.

"So it was you all along!" Fred noted. "I mean, when it wasn't Mel."

Lance growled. "I would have gotten away with it if it hadn't been for you meddling kids and your nosy . . . old . . . guy?"

Two police officers rushed over and grabbed Lance. "Thanks, we'll take it from here." They hustled Lance off as Dewey hurried in.

"Blake and Jones!" Dewey barked. "You're on in thirty seconds!" He turned and bumped into Scooby. Dewey wrinkled his nose and backed away. He whipped out some hand sanitizer and squirted it on his hands. "Your grandfather smells like a dog," he whispered to Shaggy.

"Yeah?" Shaggy snapped back. "Well, you smell like lemons."

"It's the hand sanitizer," Dewey shrugged.

"Lemons!" Shaggy yelped, looking at Scooby. "Like the Phantom!"

When they turned back to Dewey, the show's director was gone.

Onstage, Brick clapped as Chrissy wrapped up her set. "Fantastic, Chrissy, just fantastic! Wow, look at those numbers!" He turned from the scoreboard to the audience. "Up next . . . Blake and Jones!" He headed offstage as Daphne and Fred began to play.

Shaggy ran up to Brick and Colette. "Where's Dewey?"

Colette shrugged. "Like, I don't know? He's supposed to be here."

Brick looked confused. "Where the heck is he?" He put his hand up to his ear. "Well, wherever he is, he's still wearing his headset. I can hear him. He's breathing hard . . . sounds like he's running. And he's muttering . . . something about soap. But that's what he's always talking about, so . . ."

Shaggy reached up and popped out Brick's earpiece, stuffing it into his own ear. "Mind if I borrow this? Thanks!"

Shaggy and Scooby dashed down the hall and into Dewey's office. On the desk was a pile of brochures advertising the Mineralogical Society and the Soap Diamond. "Roap!" Scooby barked.

"Yeah!" Shaggy said. "That's what he's talking about! The Soap Diamond!" He grabbed one of the brochures. "The museum is right around the corner from here!"

Shaggy and Scooby raced over to the control room. K.T. whipped around to face them. "Hey! What the heck are you doing in here?!"

Velma hurried over and waved a DVD in front of them. "Guys!" she said excitedly. "Wait till you see this footage I found of—"

"No time!" Shaggy interrupted, gasping for air. "Dewey! Phantom!" He waved the brochure at her. *"Soap Diamond!"*

Shaggy pulled Velma out of the control room. Scooby followed them. In the hall, they met up with Daphne and Fred, who'd just finished singing. "Dewey's the Phantom, too!" Shaggy gasped.

"He told the police to assign everyone they have here!" Velma reminded them. "So no one would be watching the Mineralogical Society!" She led them toward the doors of the opera house. "This way!"

As they ran out of the theater, Fred turned to Shaggy. "Is Dewey saying anything?" He pointed to the earpiece in Shaggy's ear.

"Like, he just said 'Got it!' We might be too late!" They rounded a corner, and Shaggy added, "I can hear traffic! He's outside!"

Scooby pointed up. "There!"

They all looked up and saw Dewey—dressed as the Phantom—climbing down a fire escape high above the Chicago street. He had a bag slung over his shoulder.

"Dewey!" Fred cried.

"Uh . . ." Dewey said nervously. "I am the Phantom! I know nothing of this 'Dewey'!"

Shaggy pulled out his earpiece and waved it in the air. "Dude, we know it's you! You're still wearing your headset!"

"Oh, darn," Dewey muttered. In his haste, he

slipped and dropped the bag he'd been carrying. It plummeted to the ground. "No!"

Velma pointed. "The Soap Diamond!"

Scooby raced over and caught the bag in his teeth.

"Way to go, Scooby-Doo!" Shaggy said, high-fiving him.

Dewey slid down the fire escape and jumped to the ground. Then he hopped into a crazy-long red convertible.

"Ruh-roh," Shaggy and Scooby said as Dewey gunned the engine.

Dewey drove toward the gang at top speed. "I want that diamond!" he screamed.

"To the Mystery Machine!" Fred shouted.

The gang hopped into the van, and Fred hit the gas pedal. But Dewey's snazzy convertible was too powerful for them. "He's gaining on us!" Daphne cried.

Dewey cackled as he closed in on them. Fred swerved to avoid other cars. "There's no way we can lose him! He's just too fast!"

Daphne pointed at a bridge ahead that was

lifting to let boats pass on the river below. "Look out!" Fred slammed on the brakes.

"What are we gonna do?" Shaggy cried.

"Give me that bag!" Fred yelled.

CHAPTER 11

Back at the opera house, the show was almost over. "Emma Gale, everyone!" announced Brick as Emma played her last note. "Fantastic, just fantastic!"

He and the audience cheered as the votes came rolling in. "Look at those numbers! It's going to be close. And the voting closes . . . *now*!" The numbers froze. Somehow, Emma and Daphne and Fred were tied for the lead!

"Fantastic! Unbelievable! It's a tie!" Brick was beaming. "Ladies and gentlemen, we're going to need a tie-breaking encore performance! Right after these messages."

Brick waltzed backstage to congratulate Emma. "Do you have another piece you can do for the tie breaker?"

"Yeah," Emma said. "But Daphne and Fred!"

"What about them?"

"They aren't here!" someone said from the wings. "They're chasing down another Phantom."

"Another Phantom?!" Brick asked, aghast.

"Apparently, this time it's Dewey."

Brick relaxed. "I always knew there was something not right about that guy." He paused. "Emma's up after the break. We'll just have to hope Blake and Jones get back in time."

On the bridge, Dewey held the gang at knifepoint. "Hold it right there!" he demanded.

Daphne muttered, "That is the cleanest knife I've ever seen."

"Thank you," Dewey said. "Now I'll take that bag."

"Why do you want this diamond so badly, anyway?" Fred asked.

"I need it. I must complete my collection of

cleanliness-themed treasures," Dewey explained. "I've already stolen the *Ammonia Lisa* and the Sponge of Turin."

"So, that was you!" Velma said.

Dewey nodded. "But you need three things to make a collection! *Three things!* Two is just book-ends." He held out a hand to Fred. "Now. Give. Me. The. Bag."

As Dewey reached in closer, Fred tossed the bag off the bridge. "No!" Dewey cried, then leaped off the bridge after it. He landed right on a gar-bage barge.

"*Ahh!* Garbage! Unclean!" He grabbed for the bag that had fallen into the trash. "But I got the diamond! I *got it*!" Dewey opened the bag and peered inside. He shrieked. "This is a dog bone!"

Up on the bridge, Fred pulled the Soap Diamond out of his pocket and held it up. "Ooh, too bad . . ."

Scooby giggled.

Dewey looked around helplessly as sirens closed in all around him. "I would have gotten away with it if it hadn't been for you meddling kids and your filthy, germy dog!"

A police car pulled up behind the Mystery Machine. "Blake and Jones?" an officer asked.

"That's us!" Daphne answered. "We caught—"

"Dewey Ottoman," the policeman finished. "Yeah, that Brick guy called, we know everything." He pointed to the police van. "Good work! Now hop in. You tied with the violin girl so you gotta do a tie breaker! Come on, we'll take you back to the show!"

As the police sped the gang back to the opera house, Velma mused, "So, Dewey was the Phantom who faded away in that stairwell."

"Like, how did he do that?" Shaggy asked.

"I checked the camera in the stairwell. He had made a video loop of the *empty* stairwell and spliced it into the camera feed."

"Of course!" Daphne said. "So when he ran in there—"

Velma cut her off. "He activated the loop with a remote, switching the view on the monitor to the empty stairwell and making it look like he disappeared."

Fred nodded. "Very clever."

"But, you guys, you'll never guess what I found when I went through all the backstage camera footage." Velma held up a DVD. "This is gonna blow your socks off."

CHAPTER 12

As Emma was wrapping up her tie-breaker performance, the doors of the opera house burst open and the kids from Mystery, Inc. ran in.

"Come on," called Velma, pulling Shaggy and Scooby after her. "We have to make some arrangements."

Daphne and Fred hustled up to Brick. He grinned at them, then turned to the audience. "Ladies and gentlemen, Blake and Jones are here for their tie breaker! Where were you?"

"We caught another Phantom," said Fred.

"Fantastic work! Now, are you ready for your performance?" Brick clapped. "Grab your guitar, you're on!"

Fred and Daphne stepped onstage for their final performance. After they played, the crowd went wild. The scoreboard lit up as the votes climbed higher and higher. It looked as if Daphne and Fred might win!

Daphne beamed . . . until she looked past Fred into the wings. Emma and her parents were watching nervously. As much as Daphne wanted a cute new hat, she knew Emma's family needed the prize money much more than she and Fred did. She gave Fred a look, and he nodded at her.

"Say, Fred," Daphne said into the mic. "What bone will a dog never eat?"

"I don't know, Daphne!"

"A *trom*bone!" Daphne grinned, but the audience stopped clapping. Daphne continued, "Say, Fred, what vegetable do you get when you cross a dog with a rose?"

"I don't know, Daphne!"

"A collie-flower!"

The audience booed, and Daphne and Fred's score stopped moving up. Their vote counter had almost stopped.

"What the heck are they doing?" Shaggy

asked from his perch in the control room.

"They're using your jokes to throw the contest," Velma explained, "so Emma can win and her family can keep their farm."

"Rawww . . ." Scooby said. "Rhat's rute."

Onstage, Daphne continued, "What did the dog say to the tree?" She paused, then said, "'Bark!'" The audience jeered even louder.

"Well," Brick said as Daphne and Fred were booed off the stage. "That was . . . uncomfortable. All right! The voting is closed . . . NOW!" The scoreboard froze. "Fantastic! The winner, by less than a hundred votes, is EMMA GALE!" Brick patted Emma on the back, and then turned to Daphne and Fred. "Blake and Jones . . . you may not have won, but congratulations on catching all the Phantoms!"

Fred patted Brick on the back. "Not quite all." He called out, "Velma! Roll the footage!"

Every monitor in the theater lit up with footage of Brick putting on a Phantom costume. The audience gasped. The screens showed images of

Brick cutting the cable to the *Talent Star* sign moments before it crashed to the ground next to Dewey Ottoman.

"You don't understand!" Brick cried out, still grinning desperately. "I had to do it! The ratings have been dropping for years! I needed the publicity!" He looked to Daphne, Fred, and Emma for help. "You don't know what it's like, being around all you talented people all the time and being . . . *me*. What am I good at? Nothing! All I do is smile and say *fantastic* a lot! I'm pathetic!"

"Come on, Pimiento," a police officer said, escorting him offstage.

"I would have gotten away with it, if it hadn't been for—"

"Those meddling kids and their nosy dog," the officer muttered. "Yeah, we know."

"Figure this is the last one?" his partner asked.

"I dunno," the policeman said. He turned to the audience. "Is anyone else the Phantom? Show of hands?" He shrugged when no one else raised their hands. "Yeah, looks like we got 'em all."

Daphne, Fred, and Emma were left alone on the stage.

"Uh . . ." Fred said, smiling nervously out at the audience.

"So . . ." Daphne said. None of them knew how to close the show.

Suddenly, Steve Trilby, the original Phantom, jumped out of the audience and leaped up onstage. "Well, a big thank-you to all our contestants! Live from Chicago, this is Steve Trilby for *Talent Star*, saying . . . if you've got the talent, we've got the star. Good night, America!"

The audience went wild. Shaggy and Scooby jumped over the prize boxes of Fudge-A-Roni to join the others as they bowed onstage.

The show was wrapped, and so was another mystery. Just before the lights faded, Scooby barked out, "Scooby-Dooby-Doo!"

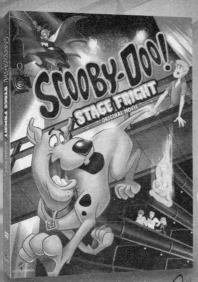

SCOOBY-DOO!
STAGE FRIGHT
ORIGINAL MOVIE

LOOK FOR IT ON BLU-RAY™ DVD AND DOWNLOAD

LOOK FOR THE LATEST SCOOBY-DOO MYSTERY MINE GAME AT A RETAILER NEAR YOU!

ZOINKS POINTS!!
ENTER THIS CODE AT
ZOINKSPOINTS.COM
TO GET FREE SCOOBY STUFF!!

SCOOBY41538

GET DOUBLE POINTS WHEN YOU REDEEM THE CODE ABOVE FROM THE MYSTERY MINE GAME AT ZOINKSPOINTS.COM

SCOOBY-DOO: TM & © Hanna-Barbera.   (s13)

ZOINKS!
MORE SPOOKY STORIES FOR FANS OF

™ and © Hanna-Barbera (s13)
SCHOLASTIC and associated logos are trademarks
and/or registered trademarks of Scholastic Inc.

SCHOLASTIC
scholastic.com
scoobydoo.com

Available wherever books
and eBooks are sold!